RISK'S REGRET

Copyright © 2022 by Loni Ree

All rights reserved. No part of this book may be reproduced in any form or by any electronic or mechanical means, including information storage and retrieval systems, without written permission from the author, except for the use of brief quotations in a book review.

Please respect the author and do not participate in or encourage piracy of copyrighted materials that would violate the author's rights.

This is a work of fiction. Names, characters, businesses, places, events, locales, and incidents are either the products of the author's imagination or used in a fictitious manner. Any resemblance to actual persons, living or dead, or actual events is purely coincidental.

Edited By: Kendra's Editing and Book Services

Cover Design By: Kate Farlow at Y'all That Graphic

❀ Created with Vellum

DIAMOND KINGS MC

Everything is bigger in Texas. The men, their bikes, their guns, and even their hearts. On the biggest ranch in West Texas, you'll find the **Diamond Kings MC**.

A group of tough, growly bikers happy with their solitary existence. Until love walks in and challenges them to the ultimate test. It's time for them to man up and accept their fate or they'll lose their soulmates forever.

Books in the series:
Risk's Regret by Loni Ree
Crow's Scorn by Misty Walker
Ruin's Revenge by Logan Chance
Sin's Sacrifice by Ella Kade
Tank's Temptation by Hope Ford
Rule's Exception by Shaw Hart
Dare's Deal by Winter Travers
Devil's Deceit by Nichole Rose

CONTENTS

"I'd rather regret the things I've done than regret the things I haven't done."

– Lucille Ball

CHAPTER 1
RISK

My plan to get a drink and ease some of the stress sitting on my shoulders flies right out the fucking window the minute I lay eyes on her. The curvy little woman sitting alone in a booth at the back of the bar blows my mind. She's the perfect bait for all the motherfucking sharks circling her, and I don't like it one bit.

Territorial thoughts rise up out of nowhere, and I wonder if I'm losing my mind. One of the little bastards gets up the nerve to approach her, and I almost laugh at the defeated look on his face as he slinks away. I glance around, giving all the hungry assholes a warning glare.

My heartbeat pounds in my ears as my hands clench at my side, and I fight the urge to twist my fingers through her long chestnut hair while I'm fucking the hell out of her. Okay. This shit is getting scary. I'm powerless to stop myself from pushing my way through the crowd, heading for the woman who just knocked me on my ass without even acknowledging me yet. What in the holy hell is going on here? If I didn't know better, I'd believe that this curvy doll just stole my heart. Fuck my life.

I stop next to her table and watch her stunning green eyes widen as I slide into the booth across from her. "I'm not interested," she huffs, but the desire swimming in her expressive eyes tells a different story.

"I wasn't asking." The words slip past my filter, and I watch her eyes narrow. Wrong fucking thing to say, dumbass. An angry red blush covers her peach-colored skin and I know it's time to backpedal.

"You just harass women for fun?" As she stares at me with one eyebrow raised, I stare back, trying to figure out how to handle this situation.

"I'm not harassing you." I shrug. "I'm trying to make your acquaintance."

"Nice try." She shakes her head. "But I'd rather we remain strangers."

A barely dressed waitress walks up, interrupting us, and I sit back to see how my girl reacts. "Can I get you anything?" My eyes water when the server leans close to me, and her sickening sweet fragrance reaches my nose. I sense an invisible wall developing between me and the curvy beauty, and I hate the distance.

"No," I growl, hoping the waitress takes the hint to get the fuck away before turning back to the girl shooting daggers at me.

"Just signal me." The clueless female pats my arm before walking away, and I barely resist the urge to wipe her touch away. Shaking my head, I wonder if I've had a brain bleed or something. My MC brother, Devil, would have a field day with me right now. Hopefully, he never finds out about this.

"You should take her up on her offer." I blink several times, trying to catch up with what I missed while having a conversation with myself. Exhaustion and stress have turned me into a dipshit.

Reaching across the scarred wooden table, I take her soft hand in mine and run my fingers across her silky skin. "You're not getting rid of me that easy."

"Lucky me," she mumbles under her breath.

For some reason, I can't walk away from the ornery female, so it's time to change strategy. Taking a deep breath, I smile at her. "Let's try this again. I'm Risk."

"A risk, or did your mother decide to name you appropriately?" She smirks and I barely resist the urge to pull her close and cover her plump lips with mine.

"Risk Long." Ignoring her flippant remark, I lean over to place a kiss on the back of her knuckles. Her emerald eyes widen as electricity fills the air around us.

"Interesting name. I could make all kinds of comments, but I'll refrain. My name is Pen." She grumbles and pulls her hand away, "Just Pen."

"Like a writing instrument?" I ask before internally groaning. I sound like a goddamn moron.

One look at the curvy little beauty and my brain went on a fucking vacation.

"Yep." She rolls her eyes and shrugs. One side of her t-shirt slips from her shoulder, giving me a glimpse of pale silky skin and causing all the blood in my body to head south of my waistband. My oxygen-deprived brain has no fucking hope of keeping up with the back-and-forth battle.

"Interesting name." I smile and feel an invisible wall coming up between us. The snarky little miss is making conversation rather difficult. "Is it short for Penny or something?"

"Or something." A lesser man might walk away at this point, but I dig my heels in for the ride. Something tells me this girl is worth the effort.

"No, I'm not from around here. No, I don't want to take a ride on your dick or anything else. No, I'm not gay." The curvy beauty pauses for a few seconds. "I think that should answer all your questions. Now that we have that out of the way, can you please leave me alone?"

That's not happening. Ever. *What*? I rub the back of my neck, wondering where these crazy thoughts are coming from. "Let me buy you a drink and we can talk." I give it one last try.

Seeing determination enter her emerald eyes, I feel my hackles rise.

"I already have a drink and I don't want to talk to you." She holds up her bottle before taking a sip. Her shoulders slump as she stares into my eyes. "Look. You're barking up the wrong tree. I'm not going to be your easy lay for the night."

"Who says I'm looking for an easy lay?" As the words leave my mouth, I see the train heading straight for me, but there's nothing I can do to avoid the collision.

"Okay, Peach." It's against my nature to give up, but a little voice in the back of my mind is ordering me to retreat. The thought of walking away from her leaves a bitter taste in my mouth, yet something tells me it's the only way to make progress with this stubborn woman. "I guess I'll see you around." Walking away from her seems to be my only option.

After riding across half of the state of Texas in one day, I need to relax and unwind, not deal with a pain-in-the-ass woman with a chip on her shoulder. I've been floundering for a while and needed some time away. I thought a solo trip would give me time to clear my mind, but this fucking excursion has only caused more frustration. Even as I tell myself to forget the curvy peach and move the fuck on, my heart tells me it won't be that easy.

I sit at the bar and force myself to ignore Pen. The television hanging on the wall has a fucking game on, so I pretend to watch it. Every now and then, I glance at the girl sitting alone in the corner, but I don't make another move. After a while, I admit defeat. This shit tastes like fucking sawdust. I slam the bottle of beer down on the bar and throw a few bills down. It's time to head up to my room. Maybe getting a little sleep will get me back to normal.

CHAPTER 2
PEN

watch the smoking hot biker disappear around the corner and instantly regret running him off. Sighing, I take one last sip of my now-warm beer and grimace. That sucks. Since the interesting scenery is gone, I guess I'll head up to my room and get some rest. This tour is draining the life out of me and I'm ready for it to end.

Seven years ago, I got the shot of a lifetime. The hugely successful rock band, Bent, needed a new bassist to replace Roman Roth. He'd been with the band since the beginning but was tired of the nomad lifestyle. Roman decided to change paths and write music instead. His departure was a miracle for me. My uncle is good friends with Hawk Knightley, the CEO of Inked Knight Records, Bent's label. Hawk offered me an audition and the rest is history. Bender Valentine, the band's lead singer, Jake Bianchi, our guitarist, and Razor Roth, the band's drummer are like three older brothers. Pains-in-the-rear, always overprotective older brothers.

For the past seven years, the band has been my family. We've spent at least eight months a year touring around the world together. Four months ago, Bender decided he'd had enough. He was ready to retire and enjoy some time away from the constant hustle and bustle of life on the road. We all supported his decision. Well, except for Louis, the band's manager. He knows the odds of finding another band that reaches our level of stardom aren't good. Actually, it's downright impossible.

Tomorrow is our last show. We're playing a benefit show for a hurricane recovery project in Houston, and then we're done. Finished.

Bender is a member of the Silver Spoon MC from the small town of Silver Spoon Falls, Texas, not far from Houston. All his brothers will be at the concert tomorrow night, then we plan to have a huge blow-out party to celebrate the end of the line. I also have an interview with London Montoya for Curvy Cuties magazine. The Silver Spoon MC President's sister approached me to be their "Curvy Cutie of the Month," and there was no way I could resist the offer.

My cellphone buzzes in my pocket and I look down to find a text from Grizz, the band's head of security.

Are you okay?

That's Grizz. Straight to the point.

Wonderful.

I message back my usual then slip my cellphone back into my pocket. It's time for me to head up and get some rest.

This is my normal routine the night before a concert. The band does a quick run-through of the upcoming show, then we all head back to the hotel to relax. I usually head down to the bar to unwind after traveling. I nurse a beer for hours and then head up to my room to sleep alone.

I step onto the empty elevator and slide my keycard into the slot. Seconds before the door closes, a masculine hand slaps between the sliding doors and stops it. I give a fake smile but attempt to ignore the tall, thin, kinda nerdy dude that steps on.

"What floor?" His voice causes the hairs on the back of my neck to stand up.

"I already chose," I tell him and wait for him to put his room key into the slot. When the doors close and he doesn't use his key, alarm shoots through me. I'm reaching into my pocket for my cellphone when he suddenly moves. The next thing I know, his arms are caging me against the steel wall.

"You are hot." His stinky breath brushes against my cheek, and I almost vomit on his shoes. I attempt to push him away, but the lanky man is stronger than he appears. A flash of steel catches my eye, and I realize he's holding a knife to my side.

Terror hits me as I wonder if anyone will save me before we hit the thirtieth floor. I'm planning to go down fighting, that's for sure. He might stab me, but the fucker isn't going to get an easy victim. Scenarios run through my mind. Maybe, I can signal one of the band employees. If they're not either asleep or out relaxing.

The elevator suddenly dings, and I breathe a sigh of relief when we stop on the floor marked *pool and conference center*. Hopefully, I don't get some family killed. "What the fuck?" Oh shit. It's the hot biker. I see him quickly scan the elevator and take notice of the situation. Risk's aqua blue eyes turn stormy as he realizes the jerk is pinning me to the back wall.

I need to warn him about the weapon hidden between the criminal and me. "He has a knife." I'm not sure who is more surprised, my attacker or would-be-savior.

Risk whips his long blond hair behind his shoulder and roars, "Motherfucker," before slamming his boot-covered foot into the other asshole's knee while simultaneously pulling the taller, skinnier man back by the neck. There's a brief scuffle, and the next thing I know, the criminal is crawling around on the elevator floor spitting out blood and teeth.

"Do you want me to call security or just take out the trash?" Risk asks. From past dealings with MC members, I know how hard it is for him to even ask. They avoid the authorities like the plague.

"Just make him go away," I mutter then back-track. "I mean, throw him out. Don't freaking hurt him."

"Don't worry, Peach. He'll survive." Risk rolls his eyes as the elevator stops on my floor.

Before my cautious mind has time to react, I make up my mind to take a risk. "I'm in room thirty-one forty-six. If you want to come by after you take care of him."

Risk's aqua blue eyes widen as a smirk crosses his handsome face. "Ready to take a risk with me?" My tongue is glued to the roof of my mouth. I nod yes before thinking better of it. "I wouldn't miss it for the world. I'll be back in a few," he tells me and holds the jerk by the neck as I step past them into the hallway. Taking a deep breath, I watch the elevator doors close. By the time I make it to my room, I'm wondering if I just made the worst decision of my life.

An hour later, I know I've been stupid. Standing on the hotel balcony, I berate myself for my stupidity. For the first time ever, I let a man get under my skin and put myself out there only to have him totally reject me. It's a good thing the big jerk never came back. At least I didn't make a fool of myself by sleeping with some jerk I just met. Even if he did save me. My cracked heart isn't listening to the bullshit, and I end up sitting on the balcony until the sun rises. I'm going to be in real good shape for the concert tonight.

CHAPTER 3
RISK

Motherfucking son-of-a-bitch. I can't get back to her floor. My keycard only works for my floor, and the front goddamn desk is no help. They refuse to ring Pen's room for me. "Sir, that guest is on our privacy list." The little bastard behind the desk smirks, and I barely resist the urge to punch the look off his face. "Sorry." He shrugs, causing me to slam my hand down on the marble counter.

I spend the rest of the night and the next morning sitting by the front door, hoping Pen walks by. An hour after check-out time, I admit to myself that she's either staying longer or I missed her. Fuck.

I had originally planned to stop and see my sister on the way back to Diamond, but I decide to head straight back. Jessie is tied up with school and won't mind. To be honest, my younger sister hates it when I interfere in her life too much.

On the ride home to the Diamond King's ranch, I attempt to clear my head and forget about the curvy little peach, but it's impossible. She's got a fucking hold on my heart.

A week later, I'm out in the back pasture using an ax for therapy. "Do you need a tampon?" Devil walks up behind me. When I turn to him, he throws me a bottle of water. Not one to look a gift horse in the mouth, I open it and drink it down in one sip.

"Do you need your ass kicked?" I fire back and watch my friend chuckle. "Fuck off." Lame but it's all I've got.

"I figured it must be that time of the month." He leans against the wooden fence and glances down at the ax in my hand. "Taking your aggression out on that firewood isn't going to work." He's right but I'll never admit it. Ever since I returned from my ride, I've been in a bad goddamn mood. Life at the ranch is getting on my nerves, dealing with my younger sister is going to give me gray hair, and I can't forget the fucking woman who stole my goddamn heart. It's been a great fucking month, all in all.

I drop the empty bottle next to the waist-high pile of wood and reach for the ax handle. "Leave me the fuck alone or I'll take it out on you," I warn my brother.

Devil ignores my threat and flips me off as he walks away. The night I got back from my week-long ride, I lost my mind and blurted out the whole story to him. It shocked my friend to his core when I admitted I'm a goddamn idiot-sandwich. I not only let the girl of my dreams slip through my fingers, but I neglected to get her fucking last name. Now, I have no motherfucking clue how to find her. Fantasies of me fucking my luscious peach fill my dreams. I'm a walking timebomb, ready to explode.

Long after the sun goes down, I stare at the clear Texas sky and rub the back of my neck. It's time to pull my head out of my ass and change the things I have control over.

Over the next few weeks, I put my plan into action. My first change is the goddamn club-house. Living in a large, converted barn with several other men was great for a while, but I'm ready to have my own place. Needing some space, I move into a travel camper on a little piece of land I bought years ago. It's only three acres, but it backs to woods on two sides and Diamond Kings' property on the other. It might take me years, but I'm building my dream spread out here.

I need to have a long talk with Jessie. Sitting at the bar in the Diamond King's clubhouse, I dial her number. "Hey, munchkin."

"I hate that name," she grumbles. "I'm nineteen years old. I've got three years of college under my belt, yet you still insist on treating me like a little kid."

Jessie is right. Our parents died in a car accident when Jessie was a sixteen-year-old senior in high school. The Diamond Kings supported me when I stepped back a little to take care of my sister. It was a learning curve, but I managed to hold down both sides of my life.

"You're the only family I have left," I remind her.

"And I love you." Jessie sighs. "But you can't run my life." It's an ongoing argument. I want to make sure she's taken care of, but my headstrong sister wants her freedom. The thought of losing my only relative terrifies me, and I have a hard time easing back on the reins.

"Why don't you come visit me over school break and we can have a long talk." I decide it's time to work this shit out before I push Jessie farther away. "You can explain your side and I'll explain mine, and we can come to an agreement. Like adults."

Jessie agrees and we end up planning for her to stay with me the entire break.

CHAPTER 4
RISK

wo weeks later, Devil and I set out to deliver horse cum to the Silver Spoon MC Ranch. The other club is made up of rich boy fuckers, but they aren't a problem for us. The do-gooders keep to themselves and pay top dollar for our services. Well, the services our studs provide.

"I never thought I'd be driving horse jizz around," I tell Devil when we pull up at the fancy-ass country-club-looking ranch. Rich fuckers. Since this shit has to stay colder than a well-digger's ass, we had to take Devil's SUV for the run.

"Life goals." He shrugs and hops out to grab the special cooler we use for these deliveries. "Stay here while I deliver the goods," he tells me when I attempt to follow him up to the large, white plantation-style clubhouse.

Devil's weird mood is confusing me. He's making jokes and acting like his usual asshole self, but there's something bugging him under the surface.

"Are you sure?" I know the trust fund babies are known for their integrity, but we usually stay together on these runs in case of trouble.

"Yep." Devil glances over his shoulder. "I have a little personal business to conduct, too." I'm curious about his *personal business* but keep my mouth shut.

Fucking thirty minutes later, I'm roasting in the hot Texas sun when Devil walks out the front door and heads for the SUV. The look in his eyes tells me his business didn't go well. I don't ask about it, figuring he'll share when he's ready.

"Want to stop by the Park Avenue Bar for a drink before we head back?" Devil asks, and I turn to stare at him. Usually, I'd be all over stopping for a beer, but ritzy digs give me hives.

"Who are you and what fucking alien took over your body?" I growl, trying to wrap my head around this turn of events.

"Oh, come on." He glances over at me and smirks. "This place isn't so bad. I mean, the scenery is very nice." My brother points at two curvy women walking down the sidewalk.

I open my mouth to speak, but the words freeze in my throat. It can't be. One chick has the same fucking hair color and walk as Pen. And the same fine, luscious ass. Holy shit. We pull past them, and I turn around in my seat to look behind us. It is my goddamn peach.

"Stop the fucking truck." Devil rears back as my shout fills the SUV but follows my order. He'll have to wait a second. I have a peach to catch.

I hop out and rush toward the two smiling women. As I step close, Pen glances up, and I watch her gorgeous green eyes widen when she recognizes me. "What are you doing here?" We both ask at the same time.

"Asshole." Her stunned expression morphs into a bored look.

"Pen, is everything okay?" the cute blonde asks. "Do I need to call Bender?"

Bender? Bender Valentine, the Rockstar? That motherfucker better not be messing with my peach.

"No," Peach reassures her friend. "It's no big deal." She points at the Trust Fund Café. "Find us a table and order me an iced tea. I'll be right in as soon as I get rid of this jerk."

"Decide you want another chance to make a fool of me?" she hisses and pokes her little finger into the center of my chest. "After you left me cooling my heels waiting, you can just bug the hell off."

"What?" Peach thinks I blew her off. What the absolute fuck? I stop in front of Pen, blocking her path. "I couldn't get back to your goddamn floor." My mouth runs away without waiting for the words my brain was planning to say. "And the fucking front desk said you had a privacy block on your room."

Her mouth rounds into a perfect O and opens and closes silently for a few seconds. "You tried to come to my room?"

"Yes!" I roar. "Now, tell me about Bender Valentine."

She blinks several times before asking, "You have no idea who I am, do you?" Holy fuck. If she's the asshole Rockstar's wife, I'm going to lose what's left of my mind.

I shake my head. "What the fuck is going on here?" Speak of the devil, I look to my right and see the angry rockstar storming towards us.

"How did you get here so quick?" Pen steps between us when he gets close.

"London called and said some club asshole was harassing you." He glares at me over Peach's head. "I was down the street at The Ritz Garage." Holy shit. This town has some crazy goddamn names.

"I told London not to bother you." Pen shakes her head. "I can take care of this."

"Uh-huh." Bender turns to glare at me. "Why are you harassing my band member?"

Now, it's me who is blinking in confusion. "Excuse me? Band member?"

Pen waves her hand in front of my face. "What is so confusing to you? That I'm his band member?" She slaps her hands down on her curvy hips. "What is wrong with me being in a rock band? I happen to be the best bassist Bent ever had."

I rub the back of my neck, trying to catch up with this crazy situation. Devil walks up and adds his two cents. "Hey, Bender. Long time."

"Not long enough," the rockstar mutters. "You need to keep this asshole away from my friend."

"Now, wait just a minute," Pen jumps in. "I'm a big girl. I can decide who I'm going to associate with," she huffs.

Pen and Bender bicker back and forth while Devil leans over to chuckle. "It's our own little soap opera, As the Motor Hums."

"It's embarrassing that you know the name of soap operas," I inform him while keeping an eye on my peach. There's no way I'm letting her disappear again.

"It's not my fault that my grandmother used to sit me in front of the television all day long." Devil shrugs.

"You hurt her, and no one will ever find your body." Bender points his finger at me then turns back to Pen. "I'll wait inside with my wife." He glares at me. "But I'll be watching. Don't make me hurt you."

This motherfucker. Devil grabs my arm. "Don't cause shit in this town," he reminds me as we watch Bender walk away. "We're on their territory." No shit. This might be Silver Spoon MC territory, but that's my fucking woman.

"I'll wait right over here." He points at the SUV parked at the curb. "While you have your little talk and all."

CHAPTER 5
PEN

otness overload. I ignore the tall, dark, and handsome biker leaning against the SUV parked at the curb and turn to deal with the hot biker holding on to my elbow. "I think we have a few things to settle."

"I don't think we do. My life is in turmoil right now." I spell it out for him. "The band retired, and I have to decide what I'm doing with the rest of my life. I don't have time for a fling."

"You need to stop making assumptions, Peach." Risk leans down to stare into my eyes. "Who said I'm looking for a fling?"

"So, what are you looking for?" My head is spinning.

"Something I never dreamed I'd ever want," Risk insists. "We can start with getting to know each other, then move on to the fun stuff."

I stare at him, silently wondering if I should jump at this chance. The cautious side of me is screaming *RUN* while my rebellious heart is begging me to take a chance. "If you want me, you'll have to work for it." I guess the hussy rebellious side just won. "Here's my number." I spout off my number and walk away. "I'm only in town for another week or so. Let's see how good you are."

The next morning, my phone dings with a text way too freaking early. Shoot, the sun barely rose an hour ago. I grab my cellphone, ready to blast whoever is brave enough to wake me up. My heart flips over in my chest when I see the unfamiliar number, then I laugh hard at the message.

Good morning, Peach. Feel like going for a ride? You'll have to ride me since my bike is back home in Diamond.

Throwing caution to the wind, I answer.

Sounds like fun.

Three little dots appear on the screen, and my heart pounds as I wait for his response.

It's not nice to tease a desperate man. Now you owe me breakfast. I'll be waiting at the 5th Ave Diner in an hour.

Taking a deep breath, I type out and send my acceptance before I'm able to talk myself out of it.

Better make it two. I just got up.

The three little dots show up again.

There are so many responses going through my mind, but I don't want to scare you off. See you in two hours.

I throw back the covers and hop out of bed, knowing two hours is barely enough time when I factor in the drive to the diner and the hour of questions I'm about to get from Bender and London.

My luck holds and I'm able to make it out of the house without my hosts catching me. I send Bender a quick text, telling him I need to run to town, then hop in my rental car before anyone sees me.

I drive into town and start looking for a parking spot near the 5th Avenue Diner. The main street is bustling with all the Thursday morning commuters. I fell in love with the small city the first time I came to visit Bender. It's the perfect combination of small-town sweetness and big-city convenience.

Last night, I laid awake most of the night debating my options. After several sleepless hours, I concluded that it's time for me to throw caution to the wind. If things go south, at least I tried. I might need a freezer full of black cherry ice cream and a truckload of tissues, but I won't regret not taking the chance.

After finding a parking space across the street from the diner, I make my way through the early morning traffic. The heavy glass and brass door screams nineteen-fifties, and I pull it open and walk into the past. I instantly melt over the adorable decor. There's black and white checked tile with stainless steel tables and red vinyl-covered seats.

The hair on the back of my neck raises while my heart races. I glance to my right and see Risk's blue eyes devouring me. Thank God, I took the time to curl my hair and apply a little bit of makeup.

"Good morning, Peach." He stands and places a soft kiss on my cheek when I reach the table.

"Good morning." Shoot. My voice sounds like a hoarse squirrel. I clear my throat and try again. "Thanks for inviting me to breakfast."

He holds out the chair for me, blowing my mind. I know that's not standard practice for bikers.

"My grandmother, Nessie, would turn over in her grave if I didn't do it," Risk whispers, and I realize I spoke my thoughts out loud.

"Oh." Come on, Pen. Get yourself together.

A waitress walks up and sets a glass of water in front of me. "My name is Georgia and I'll be your server today." I have a hard time understanding her words through the thick accent. I lean closer, hoping to hear her better. "Do you know what you want, honey? Or do you need a few minutes?" I glance up and smile when I get a good look at her. Her short, bright red hair curls around her wrinkled face, giving her the fun grandmother look. The bright blue eyeshadow and orangey-red lipstick went out of style before I was born, but it works for the adorable little woman.

"I know I need a big cup of coffee." There isn't enough caffeine in the world for me at this time of the morning. My filter doesn't work until I've had at least two cups of coffee.

"I'll be right back." The waitress smiles down at me and walks away.

I glance over at Risk and swallow. His dark blond hair hangs loose around his shoulders. I quickly shut down the fantasies of running my fingers through the long locks while he does filthy things to my body before I start drooling in the 5th Avenue Diner. He's wearing a pair of tight, faded jeans, a black t-shirt, and his cut. His trim, muscular body does all kinds of naughty things to my mind, and I feel a little over-dressed in my gray slacks and white t-shirt.

"You look hungry." He smirks.

"You have no idea," slips out before I'm able to stop it.

"Then let's get you fed." He wiggles his eyebrows and signals the waitress.

After we order, Risk asks me about myself, and I force myself to relax and answer.

"Well, I played in a few bands in college. After I graduated with a music degree, I had no idea what I'd do with the rest of my life. Then I got lucky. Bent needed a bassist and I needed a job." I hate talking about myself, but I continue. "The rest is history." I shrug.

"I'm sure there's more to it than that." He smiles. "But we can take our time getting to know each other."

I'm shocked to learn that my hot biker has a college degree. "I always loved computers, and my parents begged me to do something." He shrugs. "After graduating from A & M, I wandered around trying to decide what I wanted. Somehow, I found my way to the

Diamond Kings, and the rest is history." Risk winks, and I throw back my head to laugh.

We end up staying at the diner for two hours, just talking. It's small talk, but I end up learning a ton about Risk. He's not your typical biker. A rough criminal wouldn't give up his freedom to raise his younger sister after the death of their parents. He works full-time on the MC's ranch and does computer graphics on the side to earn extra money.

"Where's the ranch?" I ask him.

"Not too far." He smiles and reaches for my hand. "We were in town to deliver horse semen to the Silver Spoon Ranch, so I sent Devil back to Diamond and got a hotel room." Risk shrugs, and my eyebrows shoot up.

"Horse semen?" First things first. This I've got to know.

"Don't ask." He laughs at the look on my face. "It's a club secret."

"How do you get horse semen?" I need to know. "Does someone actually, uh?"

"You don't want to know," Risk assures me. "I have nightmares about it." He shudders, and I laugh at the silly look on his face. I make a mental note to google horse semen when I get back to Bender's house.

"How long are you staying in town?" Surely, he didn't stay just for me.

"However long it takes." His heated stare almost melts my panties right off my body.

Georgia comes back a while later with the bill, and Risk hands her his credit card. "Did I earn a second date?" he asks while we wait for Georgia to return with his credit card. "And maybe a ride?"

I pretend to consider it for a few seconds. "I guess."

"What are your plans for the rest of the day?" he asks as we walk out of the diner.

"I promised Bender I'd be around this afternoon." The warm Texas fall weather hits me in the face as we step outside. "We're still working on the Bent fan club and getting rid of the band-owned property." It's been a nightmare. While most of the band members are okay with retirement, our old manager and the record company are still trying to talk us into returning. We're hoping selling off the tour equipment and band-owned property will prove how serious we are.

"You still owe me a ride." He leans over and places a kiss on the side of my neck, sending electricity shooting through all the nerves in my body. "I'm going to collect it one day."

"Promises, promises," I tease him.

We make plans to have dinner Friday night before Risk walks me to my car. When he leans over to kiss me, I almost self-combust as our lips meet. My mind goes blank, and I have to lock my knees to remain standing while his tongue explores my mouth.

He pulls back and lays his forehead against mine. "I'll see you tomorrow." Risk smiles and helps me into the car. After leaning over me to grab the seatbelt, he secures it before placing a soft kiss on my lips. "Drive carefully."

I nod my head, too shocked to find words.

CHAPTER 6
RISK

nowing I need time to woo my girl, I call Devil to ask for a favor. He doesn't answer my first call so I keep redialing until the asshole answers.

"It's too fucking early," he answers. "Call back later."

"Wait," I rush to tell him before he hangs up. "I need help." My friend has never heard those words from me, and they stop him cold. "I can't keep staying at this fucking two-hundred-dollar a night hotel," I rush on to explain. "Do you know of anyone around here who could give me a place to stay for a few days?"

"Holy shit. Give me time to get coffee and make some calls," Devil growls. "I'll get back to you." Then he hangs up on me.

A couple hours later, my phone rings, and I glance down to see a pitchfork show up on the screen. Devil's idea of a little joke.

"I found you a place," Devil tells me. "I have an old friend with a place just outside of Silver Spoon Falls. Aaron uses it to get away from his old lady." My friend gives me the address and instructions for getting into the empty house.

"Nice." I get the address from Devil then hang up. After arranging to check out of the hotel, I head downtown to rent a car. The company agrees to pick it up in Diamond the next day, which is one less thing for me to arrange. It feels foreign to drive on four wheels, but I manage to drive back to Diamond in record time. I rush to my place and pack a bag and my computer before hopping on my bike. On the ride back to Silver

Spoon Falls, I run through my plans. I can work from there for a week or two before things get tricky. Surely, that's long enough to win over my peach. It's almost dark by the time I make it to the secluded little place.

It isn't luxurious like Devil's place, but it will definitely work for what I have in mind.

Once I'm settled, I text Peach.

Do you mind a change of plans?

Her reply comes back quickly.

What do you have in mind?

Smiling, I put my plan into action.

I'm cooking dinner. I'll pick you up at six. Wear comfy clothes.

She sends back a thumbs up, telling me it's a go.

After a quick run to the grocery store in town, I come back to the house and throw together Nessie's famous spaghetti sauce. I set the crockpot for low and get to work on the rest of my plans.

At a quarter to six, I hop on my bike and head out to Bender Valentine's place to pick up my girl.

I pull up in front of the white and green plantation-style home and shake my head. My girl is used to the finest in life, and I can't provide anything close to this. Don't get me wrong, I'm not destitute, but I'm also not rolling in dough.

I push that worry to the back of my mind and walk up to knock on the front door. I'm not surprised when Bender Valentine opens it and steps out onto the porch. "I want a word with you." He glares at me.

"If you hurt my little sis, they won't ever find your body." I respect his words, but I refuse to let the rich boy get the upper hand.

"Not that it's any of your business, but she's mine." I leave it there. The fucker can figure out the rest on his own.

"She's almost ready." His glare loses some of its heat. "I only see one helmet." He points at my bike. "Either borrow one for her, or I'll drive her to your place."

This fucker. "I appreciate you letting us borrow one." I'm glad my peach has someone to look out for her. Soon, I'll convince this fucker that I'm taking over the job.

I follow him in the front door and almost swallow my tongue. Fuck, she's perfect. "Hi." Pen smiles and walks toward me. My cock turns to stone while my eyes roam over her luscious body. She's wearing tight-ass jeans and a dark purple shirt that gives me a good peek at the delicious curves beneath.

"Hi, Peach." I wrap my arms around her soft hips and pull her close. "You look great."

Bender makes gagging noises and walks away as Pen smiles up into my eyes. "So do you."

"Here." He returns with a helmet and shoves it into my hands. I know the asshole is head over heels in love with his old lady, so I don't let his protectiveness toward my girl piss me off.

Luckily, the drive back to my temporary digs is short. Having my luscious peach pressed against my back causes problems of the painful kind down below. My zipper might leave a permanent indentation on my hard cock if I don't give it some relief. Fast.

I help Pen off the bike and follow her to the front door.

"You rode like a pro," I tell her, hoping to ease her fears. She told me at breakfast that she hasn't been on a bike in forever.

"Thanks." My peach smiles up at me. "It took Bender a long time to convince me to give it a try."

The thought of her holding on tight to another man pisses me the fuck off, but I let it go since I know she views the fucker as a brother.

As we walk, I attempt to adjust my hardness, but the fucker is wedged in. Fuck. Hopefully, my peach doesn't notice me dancing around like I have ants in my goddamn pants.

I open the door for her and she stops to gasp. "Something smells so good. I'm starving."

"I have something you can snack on," I mutter under my breath, but it comes out louder than I intended.

"Maybe after dinner." Pen looks over her shoulder and winks, causing my cock to throb with anticipation.

Pulling my head out of my ass, I point to the sofa. "Have a seat and I'll get us something to drink." I sound like a fucking pussy-whipped douchebag, but I don't care. Winning over my girl is worth any amount of pain.

"Why don't we get something together, and I'll help you put dinner on." She takes my hand, relaxing me.

After we serve our plates, I lead her onto the back deck. "Do you mind eating on the back deck?" As the sun fades from the sky, the temperature cools to a tolerable level.

"Not at all." When she smiles, my heart gives a weird jerk in my chest. "I love being outside."

We eat in silence. All my plans to woo my curvy peach fled my mind the moment she sat across from me. "This is fabulous." Pen points to her half-empty plate.

"Thank you," I mumble and watch her bring a bite to her mouth. As her juicy lips close over the fork, dirty images overtake my mind.

"What's wrong?" Pen glances at me and frowns. "You're moaning."

Fuck. "I was envisioning your lips wrapped around my cock." That wasn't what I intended to say.

"Oh." Her mouth opens and closes silently. I spend the next few moments trying to figure out how to salvage the situation. Pen takes a deep breath and blurts out, "I'd like to make that happen." What? My brain is processing her words when she adds, "Now."

She doesn't have to ask me twice. Standing, I reach for her hand. "Are you sure?"

"Never been surer." Pen takes my hand and follows me inside. The moment we clear the sliding door, she turns and wraps her arms around me. My mind short-circuits as I kiss her soft lips.

CHAPTER 7
PEN

'm done playing it safe. Throwing caution to the wind, I fall into his kiss. His strong arms wrap around me, pulling me against his hardness. And boy is it hard. I groan into his mouth while trying to ignore the little voice in the back of my mind that's ordering me to give him some warning. Holy heck this is moving fast.

I pull back to stare into his blue eyes and find enough heat there to melt my clothes off my body. Wrapping my arms around his neck, I take a deep breath, preparing to blurt out my little secret. "There's one thing you should know before we go any further. I don't have experience."

Risk blinks several times as his eyes narrow. "Much experience or no experience?"

"A big ole zilch." How freaking embarrassing. A twenty-seven-year-old hard rock bassist with absolutely no sexual experience.

He stares at me for several seconds. "I hope you know I'm never letting you go," he roars before lifting me against his muscular chest. "You're fucking beautiful, Peach. And all fucking mine." He runs his tongue up the side of my neck, leaving goosebumps in his wake.

When he sets me on my feet next to the bed, worry blasts through my mind, but I resist the urge to cut and run. "You're worth the risk." I smirk and watch him throw back his head to laugh.

"I'm not sure how I got lucky enough to get a second chance with you, but I plan to make the most of it." He lifts my shirt over my head. "My biggest regret is screwing up the first chance I got with you."

I shiver as he places little kisses along my collar bone. "Definitely don't want you to have regrets." The words fall from my lips as I let him tear the rest of my clothes from my body.

Dropping back onto the bed, I watch him shed his own clothes. Risk pulls his jeans and underwear down, giving me my first glimpse of his equipment. Man, he is loaded. My heart pounds in my chest as I stare at his huge erection bouncing against his flat stomach.

"That's big." Great. I sound like a freaking teenager.

"Why, thank you." He looks into my eyes and winks. "I'm glad you approve."

To take my mind off the huge dick coming for my unused girly parts, I stare at the tattoos covering his chest and arms. Wetness drips between my thighs, causing me to squirm and rub them together.

"Are you having second thoughts?" Risk gives me another chance to back out, but I'm in this for the long haul.

"I'm ready to take the risk." I shake my head, watching him reach down to stroke his erection.

"I can see you're going to keep me on my toes." He prowls over to the bed and leans down to kiss my nose. "I'm one lucky motherfucker."

"You could get lucky if you'd get to work." I slide my hand along his abdomen down to his hard cock. My thumb traces the head, spreading wetness around.

"You don't have to ask me twice."

He closes his lips around one of my nipples and sucks before moving to the other side to give it the same treatment. "I like that," I breathe out, not sure what all I'm babbling.

"I hope you like this more." Risk kisses his way down my body. Each time he stops to place a tiny bite on my skin, I fall a little further under his spell. The gruff biker treating me like spun glass is a huge turn-on. "My juicy peach." His tongue teases my belly button before he moves to the important parts.

"Once I fuck this perfect body, I won't ever let you go," he warns. "You'll be mine forever." He slips his hand between my legs and pulls them open for his mouth to explore.

"And you're mine. Only mine," I let him know where I stand. His eyes roam over my body until his gaze reaches my eyes. Holding my eyes captive, he slides a huge finger into my slit. A slight sting brings tears to my eyes, but I ignore the discomfort and force my inner muscles to relax. "You're goddamn tight."

He nips my clit with his teeth, then soothes the ache with his tongue while his finger presses deeper. "Another winner," I compliment him, concentrating on the sparks of pleasure dancing up my spine.

"Good to know." He curls his finger and hits a spot that causes my eyes to fall shut as my back arches. Fireworks blast behind my closed lids while I ride the wave of pleasure.

"Mine," he hisses against my opening before sliding a second finger into my pussy. Risk slowly strokes the fire until I detonate.

"Oh my God." I gasp and come around his fingers.

Risk crawls up my limp body, leaving little kisses in his path. "Let's see if we can do even better."

He slides the tip of his hard cock through the wetness at my opening, then presses it in. I'm glad the years of using my little battery-operated friend have helped ease this first time. My intimate muscles still resist his invasion, but I don't feel any sharp pain. He pumps his hips, driving his cock all the way. "Fuck. I love you," he groans, and I stiffen in shock. I'm not sure if it's the words or the feeling of being filled to the brim that gets me.

"Please move," I whimper and dig my nails into his ass cheeks.

He doesn't make me beg. His hips pick up speed while I hold on for the ride. When Risk reaches between us to rub circles on my clit, the fireworks return. Only this time, I see every color of the rainbow as I come. "I love you," roars through my mind, and I'm not sure whether the words slip past my throat or not.

Risk slows his thrusts, letting me ride out my orgasm. "You're fucking beautiful when you come calling my name." He circles his hips. "I want to see another time." Holy cow. Three orgasms in one night is asking for a lot, but he pulls it off.

The third time I come, he lets go and comes with me. His erections jerks as warmness fills me. Oops.

Sometime later, I wake up surrounded by his warmth. His spicy, masculine fragrance wraps around me, sending another wave of hunger shooting through my blood, but the soreness down below warns me that getting too adventurous right now isn't a good idea.

"Good morning." He turns me on my back and crawls over me before kissing me within an inch of my life. Morning breath and all.

"Good morning." I sigh once the Risk-induced brain fog clears.

"I'm going make coffee." He rolls out of bed, giving me a show. His muscular back and perfect ass cause me to rethink my earlier decision. Surely, one more round wouldn't hurt anything. "You might want to check your phone. The fucker has been vibrating on the floor for a while now, but I wanted to let you sleep in."

Oh, shoot. Bender probably has the authorities out looking for me. Oops. I dig around on the floor and find my cellphone in my pants pocket.

Sure enough, three missed calls from Bender, two missed calls from London, and ten total texts. I quickly dial London's number, figuring my friend will be easier to calm down than her old man.

"Please tell me you're alright," she begs.

"Of course, I'm alright," I reassure her. "Risk is my Bender." My friend knows I've been hoping to find what she has with the rockstar.

"Then please tell me you're sore and well-loved." My friend laughs. "It will make up for the blasting you're about to get from Bender."

"I am," I reassure her a second before my pseudo big brother's voice comes on the line.

"Penelope Sky Rocha. Where the hell are you?" It's bad. He used my full name.

I watch Risk holding back laughter as he listens to me trying to reassure Bender. "I promise everything is okay."

After several rounds of fussing from him and apologies from me, Bender finally sighs. "If you ever scare me like that again, I'm locking you up and throwing away the key." I hear London in the background, reassuring her man that I have someone else to take care of me now.

In my heart, I let go of all my fears and reservations. It's time I take a risk and give Risk a chance.

He asks me to stay at his place in Diamond so we can get to know each other. Knowing how difficult a long-distance relationship is, I agree to us moving in together, then make arrangements to bring some of my things to Diamond.

When I get my first look at the travel camper Risk lives in, I put my foot down. I'm not rich, but I do like my creature comforts.

"I could buy us a house," I tell him over breakfast.

"Hell no, my woman isn't buying a house for me," he growls, and the determined look in his blue eyes tells me this is one argument I won't win. "I'm not rich like your rockstar friend, but I do have money in the bank. I was already planning to build a house on some land I own. We'll just move up the timeframe." He explains that he's been working on plans for a modest home on a bit of property that borders the MC compound. After my proud biker puts his foot down, he drives me out to the property and we both agree it's perfect.

In the meantime, we'll look for a little place to rent since the camper is a hard no for me.

CHAPTER 8
RISK

You expect me to drop everything and go away with you?" Pen glares at me, and I take a sip of my coffee before shrugging. She's been staying at the cabin with me for several weeks. Things are moving fast but not fast enough for me. After all, Devil always tells me I was born without patience.

Needing to make my move, I arranged a little getaway while my peach slept in. I have big plans for us. A week of relaxing at Devil's fancy getaway in the woods. When the time is right, I intend to ask Pen to marry me. There's a ring hidden in my bag if things go as planned.

"You just complained last night that you're bored," I remind her. "I thought we could kill two birds with one stone." She pours herself a cup of coffee before sitting on my lap.

"I'm going to find something to do with my time," she assures me and wiggles a little, sending hunger shooting through my soul. My cock turns to stone as her soft ass cheeks cradle it.

"I borrowed Devil's fishing cabin for the weekend. We can spend some time alone and fuck like rabbits."

"One." Pen looks over her shoulder and glares. "We don't have to get away to fuck like rabbits. My sore kitty can attest to that." She's right, but I look forward to spending alone time with my girl. "Two." She frowns. "A fishing cabin? Do I look like the roughing it type?" She points at the modest place we've been staying with a raised eyebrow. "This place is as rough as I get. My idea of roughing it is a hotel with an outdoor pool."

I pull her into my arms and smile down into her emerald eyes. "Don't worry. I won't let your gorgeous ass rough it, much." After giving her soft ass a little smack, I kiss the side of her neck and tell her, "Go pack."

"We really need to talk about your insistence on ordering me around," Pen calls over her shoulder.

"That's the perfect thing to do. At the fucking cabin," I tease.

"If you keep this up, I'll be smothering you with a pillow." She sticks her head around the corner.

"I like it kinky, but that's a little too kinky for me."

After packing, we load our stuff into Pen's SUV. When she decided to stay with me for a while, she had it shipped from California with some of her belongings. It comes in handy since there's no way we could get all the shit she's packing on my bike. Goddamn, she doesn't fucking pack lightly.

Three hours later, we pull up outside Devil's "fishing" cabin. "This isn't a cabin." Pen blinks and stares at the large two-story structure. "It's a freaking mansion."

I open the car door and reach for my girl's hand. "Come on. I'll show you around."

After a quick tour, we unpack our supplies, and I cook lunch while she relaxes on the back deck.

"Feel like a swim after lunch?" I ask my peach.

"Of course." She looks around the backyard. "But where's the pool?"

"Oh, city girl. You have so much to learn."

"Can we skinny dip?" Pen looks over her shoulder and wiggles her eyebrows as we walk down the path leading to Devil's private lake.

"Hell yes," I answer, staring at her luscious ass in the skimpy two-piece swimsuit. All the dirty things I'm going to do to her sweet body run through my mind.

We drop our things on the dock, and I turn to my peach. "That is one hot bikini, but I would prefer to see it laying on the dock."

She gives me a sultry look before reaching back to untie the bands. Her sweet tits pop out as she lets the top slide down her arms. I slide my shorts off while she pulls the tiny bottoms down her silky legs. Once she drops both pieces onto the deck, Pen turns to me and points at the hot pink material. "Look as good as you imagined?" she asks.

"Sassy little peach," I tell her before dropping back onto the deck lounger. "Come sit on my lap and let me taste you."

She wanders over to me and slips one silky leg over my lap. Her fingers grip my shoulders as she slides down. My cock nestles between her legs while her luscious tits tease me. I lean forward and wrap my lips around one of the hard little nubs.

CHAPTER 9
PEN

slide my hand down his muscular chest and reach for his erection. A shiver runs down my spine when he bites down on my nipple before sucking it into his warm mouth.

Risk reaches between my legs to press his thumb against my clit, causing wetness to seep from my opening to his lap. When he spreads my legs wider and picks me up by my hips to slide me down his cock, I almost come from the sensations bombarding me. My inner muscles stretch around his erection as I move my hips faster.

"What are you doing?" I squirm as he slides his thick finger up my butt crack to play with my other hole.

"Making you feel good," he groans while pressing his finger past the opening. "Just tell me to stop if you don't like it."

I'm too overwhelmed by his touch to answer as he presses a little deeper.

"Later, we'll explore this more." He gives my butt cheek a squeeze while nibbling on the side of my neck. Risk lifts his hips up to meet my downward movements.

"More. More." His movements speed up as I beg. When he arches his hips, sending his erection impossibly deep, pleasure blasts through me and I come, screaming his name.

"I love you, Peach." He rubs light circles on my back while my breathing slows to normal. He kisses the side of my neck and whispers, "I want you forever. Will you marry me?" The words send my heart into overdrive as I sit up to stare into his eyes.

"Married?" Oh my. It's so soon.

"Either that or I can kidnap you and keep you for my love slave." He shrugs.

"I guess you talked me into it. I've always wanted to be a love slave." I almost fall off his lap when Risk starts tickling me. He kisses me until I melt against his strong body. When he finally lets me come up for air, I lay my head on his shoulder and listen to his steady heartbeat.

"You can be both," he offers, and it takes me a second to remember what we're talking about. "I'd like to have my ring on your finger before you pop out the first kid, but I'm open to the whole love slave thing, too."

He's so eloquent. "It sounds like we're on the same page, then."

Once we get back to the cabin, he pulls a huge diamond ring from his bag. "I want to add the wedding band to this as soon as possible," Risk tells me while slipping it on my finger.

We spend the rest of the weekend trying to come up with a way to have a wedding ceremony with all our friends and family present. The two MCs aren't rivals, but they also aren't exactly besties.

While I'm stressing over wedding plans, my future career plans fall into place. A private grade school close to Diamond is looking for a music teacher. Bender and his President, Cash Montoya, take it upon themselves to put in a good word for me. The next thing I know, the school principal is calling to offer me the position. I'm not crazy about using my friends and family to get a job, but I don't look a gift horse in the mouth. It's one less thing for me to worry about.

Between my savings and Risk's savings and income, we're nowhere near destitute, but we will need two steady incomes in the future. Especially if we have all the freaking kids he's planning.

Over the next few weeks, we settle into the small home on the back edge of the MC land. Risk has been introducing me to his MC brothers one at a time. I'm not going to lie; meeting the huge freaking bikers is intimidating. My former career taught me to deal with testosterone, but I've never seen so much in one place.

Then there's Devil. Every now and then, I see something flash through his eyes that tells me he isn't as hard as he appears. I get the impression he's hiding something, but I keep my thoughts to myself.

Risk's sister, Jessie, comes to stay with us for her school break, and I instantly fall in love with the younger woman. She's smart, snarky, and doesn't let her brother get away with anything. We end up spending the entire week getting to know each other and ganging up on her brother.

"I wish you didn't have to leave." I hug her close while Risk loads her suitcase into the trunk of her car.

"I'll be back," she promises me. "I have to come and rescue you from all the testosterone overload around here." The female version of my hot biker grins at me.

"You don't need to worry about anything male." Risk hugs his little sister close. "Not until you're at least forty-five."

"Good God." She rolls her eyes. "I need to get going." Jessie gives me and Risk each another hug before hopping in her car and rolling down the window.

Risk opens his mouth to speak, but she stops him. "I know. Don't stop for strangers, keep the doors locked, and call you when I get back to my dorm."

"I'm glad you have the routine down." He kisses her cheek.

CHAPTER 10
RISK

ome over here and sit that pretty pussy on my face." I point at my chin and watch the adorable pink blush move up my girl's neck.

I rented this place for Pen and me when we got back from Devil's lake house, then kicked the plans for our new home into overdrive. The architect assures me they will break ground on our new house within a few weeks. He's thinking six to nine months and we should be able to move in. *Just enough time to knock up my little peach* runs through my mind, and I realize the thought doesn't scare me in the least. Instead, I'm looking forward to seeing my curvy little peach grow large with our child.

Until the house is ready, we'll stay in this small one-bedroom home on the back of the ranch property. It's been empty since the last ranch hand moved out several months ago. The MC keeps the little home "just in case," and my situation definitely qualified since I wasn't moving my peach into either the clubhouse or that little travel trailer I had been using.

"If you want this," Pen pulls her t-shirt over her head before pointing down her luscious curves, "then you'll have to catch me." She hops up and hurdles over the sofa before turning to throw her shirt at me. "Old man." I watch her make a beeline for the bedroom and feel my cock turn to stone. Oh, hell no. My little peach isn't getting away from me. She loves using that term with me, and my heart turns over with happiness each time I hear it.

As I chase her down the hall, we leave a trail of clothes in our path. Pen runs into the bedroom and tries to close the door, but I jam my foot against the wood, stopping her. She squeaks when I wrap my hand around her elbow and pull her curvy body against mine. "I caught you," I tease and run my tongue up the side of her sweet neck. Pen turns in my arms and pinches my side. "Ow." I rub the little injury and smile against her soft lips. "That's not nice."

"You weren't very nice when you tormented me all evening long. I'm just getting my revenge," she mumbles, reaching between us to run her fingers lightly over the head of my cock. That's true. Watching her emerald eyes darken with hunger was the highlight of our long evening. I almost come when she drops to her knees in front of me. My curvy peach smiles up at me and winks. "Hold on for the wild ride."

"Fuck," I groan as she sucks my cock to the back of her throat. My knees turn to Jell-O and I end up leaning against the fucking door to remain standing. Her soft hand wraps around my balls and gently massages, causing my dick to grow impossibly harder. When she runs her talented tongue around the sensitive head, my eyes roll back.

"I need to feel your luscious pussy wrapped tightly around my cock."

Pen leans down to give my balls a light lick before sitting back on her knees. "You're the boss."

"Don't you forget it." I smile and reach down to lift her curvy body against mine before tossing her onto the bed. I watch her killer tits bounce as she lays back to run her finger along the pale skin above her pussy.

"Come boss me." She slips her finger into her wet pussy before holding it up to me. "Want a taste?"

"Fuck yes." I reach for her hand and suck her juices off her finger. I pull Pen to her feet. "I've been dreaming of you sitting on my face all night long."

For once, she doesn't fight me. Lying back, I reach for her leg and pull it over my shoulder. "Oh, my goodness," she groans as I wrap my hands around her luscious ass cheeks and pull her down over my head. I devour her pussy while she holds on to the headboard and grinds her luscious pussy on my face.

Turning my head to the side, I bite down gently on the inside of her thigh before running my tongue over the area. "I might just stay here forever." Spreading her pussy lips wide open, I slip my tongue into her wet hole, and it takes all my control not to come as her flavor hits my tongue.

"Make me come," my peach begs, and I can't deny her anything. I rub her sensitive clit with my thumb and swallow her down as she comes all over my face.

She slides down my body and reaches between us to squeeze my cock. "Can I ride your cock now?" Holy fuck. I almost come from her words alone.

"I'll take your silence as a yes." Pen presses her wet opening against my hardness and then slowly impales herself. Her silky heat envelops my dick, and I nearly lose my mind. Her curvy thighs grip my hips tightly as she picks up her pace.

I whimper when she pauses. "I want to make this last all night long." She leans over and sucks on the side of my throat. I'm sure she's leaving a deep purple bruise to get revenge for the hickeys I've been leaving on her neck for weeks.

"I'll fuck you all night long," I promise and wrap my hands around her hips. "Now move that beautiful ass." She jerks and glares down at me when I smack her left ass cheek, but the warm wetness running down my balls tells me she loves the little spanking.

I watch her juicy tits bounce as she lifts herself up and down on my cock. When I play with her clit, my peach detonates. Her inner muscles clench around my shaft, sending intense pleasure shooting through my veins. It's time she knows my intentions.

"I plan to knock you up tonight," I growl and hold her hips tightly as I shoot my cum deep into her pussy.

"Well, get to it." She flops onto my chest and groans.

"I think that's the first time you've ever agreed with me without arguing," I tell her. "Life doesn't get any better than this."

"How do you always come up with the perfect words to both melt me into a puddle of goo and piss me off at the same time?" She pinches my left nipple. We're going to have to work on her tendency to pinch. Or, at least, teach her where I want to be pinched.

"I'm just that good." I wrap my hand around the back of her neck and pull her down for my kiss. "I fucking love you more than I ever thought possible." Staring into her eyes, I spill my guts. "Finding you was the best thing that ever happened to me."

"I swear." She shakes her head. "You love to turn me to mush with your sweet words."

"That's because I love to see you melt." Reaching between us, I press hard on her clit while watching her emerald eyes turn black. "I know we've been trying to decide whether to have the wedding here or in Silver Spoon Falls, but I have a better idea." I can't wait to give her my last name, and the wedding planning is getting out of control. "Will you let me take you to Vegas for a quicky wedding? I want to make you mine without dealing with the drama of having a wedding in Diamond or Silver Spoon Falls."

"I can't wait to be your wife. Something simple and uncomplicated sounds wonderful." My curvy peach shifts above me, and my cock instantly hardens as she smiles down at me. "I love you, too. Now, knock me the fuck up." She doesn't have to ask me twice.

CHAPTER 11
RISK

nce my girl agrees to a quicky ceremony in Las Vegas, I get my ass into gear and make it happen. "I can't believe we're getting married tonight." Pen squeezes my hand tight as the car pulls up in front of the hotel. "And I'm so sorry Jessie couldn't come."

"I can't fucking wait to make you mine." Leaning over, I kiss her forehead, then hop out and help her from the car. "I'm not waiting two or three more weeks until my sister can get away," I remind her. "She can come to visit us once her semester winds down." The attendant walks over for our bags while I lead my girl into the busy lobby.

We're waiting for an elevator when some soon-to-be-dead motherfucker reaches for my woman and gives her a goddamn hug. "Hello, beautiful. What are you doing in Vegas?" he asks, and I don't give my peach time to answer before I slam my fist into his face.

"Risk!" Pen gasps while the fucker rights himself.

"What the fuck?" he roars, coming toward me. Two massive assholes rush toward us, and I know my goose is cooked, but there's no way I'm letting another man get away with touching my woman right in front of me.

"Stop." Pen jumps between us, looking back and forth between us. "Please."

The asshole holds his hand up to the other two, stopping them dead in their tracks. "Pen, who is this asshole?" He turns to my girl, rubbing the bruise already forming on his left cheek.

"Hawk, this is my fiancé, Risk Long." Then she takes my hand and holds it tight. "Risk, this is my former boss and the CEO of Inked Knight Records, Hawk Knightley."

I narrow my eyes, waiting to see what the asshole does. He surprises me and holds out his hand. "I didn't mean any disrespect. I've known Pen since she was a little girl."

I accept his apology and shake his hand. "From now on, you need to remember she's a woman. My woman."

Pen groans next to me but doesn't interrupt us. "Fair enough," the asshole agrees and signals for the other two to step back. They position themselves a few feet away and pretend to ignore our conversation.

"We're here to get married," Pen tells him, and I watch his eyes widen. "Tonight," she adds.

"Does Bender know you're eloping?" This fucker is determined to piss me off.

"Of course," Pen assures him. "He wanted to be here, but the wedding planning got out of hand. We decided to take the easy route and come here and elope. We want simple."

"Well, I'd like to do something to celebrate your wedding." My eyes narrow, waiting for him to finish explaining. Talk about a one-eighty. He was ready to murder me and hide the body a few moments ago. "I'll arrange for you to stay in the honeymoon suite." He smiles at Pen. "As my wedding present."

The urge to reject his offer sits on the tip of my tongue, but I fight it when I get a glimpse of the happiness on Pen's face. "Thank you," ends up coming out of my mouth instead, surprising the shit out of me and Hawk Knightley.

"Yes, Hawk." Pen steps over to him and gives him a hug. "Thank you." While I'd like to beat the fucker again, I don't want to start off my marriage with my old lady pissed at me.

Within five minutes, he's arranged for our new digs, and we're on our way up the private elevator. "This was so nice of Hawk," Pen gushes, and I grind my teeth together to hold my real opinion back. "Is something wrong?" She glances over at me as we step into the massive suite.

"My blood pressure hasn't come down since I saw that asshole touching you," I tell her honestly.

My curvy peach turns and wraps her arms around my waist. "I promise you," she stares into my eyes, "there has never been anything between me and Hawk or any other man associated with the band. I saved myself for my soulmate. You."

Her soft hand reaches between our bodies to grip my aching cock through the denim, and my mind shuts down. I cover her lips with mine and thrust my tongue into her waiting mouth while tearing at my clothes. Pen steps back and slowly pulls her shirt over her head. When she unhooks her bra and lets her luscious tits fall free, my mouth waters.

I lean down and close my lips around her nipple while helping her out of her tight jeans. I lift Pen's sweet body against mine and press her back to the wall. She wraps her silky legs around my waist and sighs, "I love you," against the side of my neck as I sink into her wet pussy.

"I love you, too." Her satiny tightness squeezes my cock tightly, and I nearly come on the first thrust. Her soft curves cushion my hips as I pound into her velvety heat while our tongues duel. When her silky walls tremble around my shaft, I lock my knees to remain on my feet. Our cries echo around the room as we come together.

I ease Pen to her feet and glance around at our clothes strewn around the large room. "I'm loving this suite."

"Me too." She pushes her hair back from her heart-shaped face. "But now we have to shower and get ready fast if we're going to make it to our wedding on time."

It's close, but we end up rushing through the chapel door with ten minutes to spare. Thirty minutes later, the Elvis impersonator tells me to kiss my bride. He doesn't have to tell me twice.

"I love you, Mrs. Long." I hug her curvy body close.

"I love you, too, Sean Risk Long." My full name falling from her lips sends shivers up my spine as she smiles up into my eyes. "You're the best risk I've ever taken."

"Cute. Real cute." I smack my old lady's ass before throwing her over my shoulder and racing for our honeymoon suite.

EPILOGUE

PEN

'm going to literally explode if this baby gets any bigger. Glancing down, all I see is a huge watermelon covered with black fabric. Seeing my feet is just a distant memory.

The sound of the garage door opening tells me my relief is about to come through the door. Woofwoof, our guard dog-slash-big rug, lifts his head and gives a little bark before rolling over and going back to sleep.

"DADDY!" Logan screams at the top of his lungs, causing me to wince and the dog to whimper.

"Yes," I pick up the two-year-old miniature of my husband and kiss his sweet cheek, "Daddy is home." *Thank God,* I add under my breath. As much as I love our firstborn, he has two speeds—asleep and full throttle—and two volumes—deafening and ear-splitting.

"Honey, I'm home." Risk walks up and places a kiss on the back of my neck. "How are my little ones doing?" He pats my huge stomach and smiles down at me while reaching for Logan.

"One is splitting my ears, and the other is playing basketball with my bladder." It's my usual response.

"Great." Risk winks. "Just a normal day then." I barely resist the urge to kick him in the balls. Smug jerk.

My husband wraps his arm around my rapidly disappearing waist. "I know carrying this little girl while trying to keep up with this little dude," he points his head toward our toddler, "is insanely hard and frustrating, but they couldn't have a better mother." Tears fill my eyes. Freaking pregnancy hormones.

"Thank you," I blubber against his strong chest.

"Did you just wipe snot on my shirt?" he teases, and I smack his arm while shaking my head *no*. Risk leans over and gives Woofwoof a pet before placing Logan on the floor.

"I talked to Bender a little while ago." That's not a shock. My husband and pseudo-big brother have become close since we got married. "Since you and London both need a night out, he's coming pick you up and dropping both of you off at the movie theater. Then he'll drive you ladies out to dinner but stay hidden in the background. You won't even know he's there."

"What about Lacey?" Surely, Bender isn't going to drag his daughter around on this expedition. Like Risk, Bender is a great father, but his little one is quite a handful. Even busier and louder than Logan.

"I'm on toddler duty." Risk winks. "We're going to have two kids in a few months." He shrugs like taking care of two children under three is no big deal. "I figure I'll get good practice tonight." Boy will he ever.

"Thank you." I lean up and kiss his lips. "I could really use the night out."

"Go get ready. I'm going to get this guy some dinner." He doesn't have to tell me twice.

While Risk takes our hungry toddler to the kitchen, I race up the stairs. Okay, I waddle up the stairs and head for our bedroom. When we designed the house, I wasn't sure I'd like having my bedroom on one side of the house and all the kids' rooms all the way on the other side, but my husband was so right. The distance is a great sound barrier.

Three years of marriage and a young child haven't slowed down our desire for each other, and I figure we're going to be *fucking like rabbits* well into our nineties.

Four hours later, I drag my exhausted body through the garage door with Bender right behind me. What sounded like a great idea a few hours ago turned out to be an expedition in torture. Getting up and down the steep movie theater stairs when you can't even see your feet and have no bladder control sucks. London and I gave up about seventy-five percent through the movie. Since we were both starving, we decided to go through the nearest drive-thru instead of waiting for service in a sit-down restaurant.

I walk quietly around the corner and find Risk sound asleep on the sofa with a toddler under each arm and the large Rottweiler snoring on the floor at his feet. The two kids are wide awake and watching a cartoon on the large flat-screen television. "MOMMY!" Risk nearly jumps out of his skin when Logan screeches.

"Shhh." Lacey holds her finger up to her lips. "You's too loud." She looks over my shoulder and smiles wide. "Right, Daddy?"

Bender chuckles behind me. "Right, sweetpea. Come on, we need to get Mommy home. She's asleep in the car." He calls over to Risk, "I'll call you tomorrow to get an update on how the night went."

"Sounds good." My husband yawns. "But next time, I'm driving the women around."

"We'll see." Bender laughs and hugs his daughter close.

After Bender and Lacey leave, I help my husband put Logan to bed. We have the usual three stories and two trips to the bathroom before he's ready to pass out. Our busy son is sound asleep before we even leave the room.

"How did the night go?" I sit on the edge of the bed and sigh as he pulls off my sneakers and begins rubbing my tired feet.

"Great." He shrugs. "The fire department only came once," he jokes, and I stick my tongue out at him before dropping back on the soft comforter. I groan as he works the arch of my foot. "You're real funny," I grumble. So, I accidentally set the kitchen on fire one time. It was a small fire, and my quick-thinking husband put it out quickly before there was any damage.

"Seriously," Risk lays down next to me and rubs my huge baby bump, "it was fine. The kids played, I chased them, Lacey cut Woofwoof's hair, and then we watched television."

"Poor Woofwoof." My husband let his sister go wild when our child turned one. Nannie Jessie, as we call her, bought Logan a Rottweiler puppy. Our headstrong son took one look at the little animal and started shouting, "Woof, woof!" Somehow, the name stuck, and everyone calls the poor animal Woofwoof.

"Poor Woofwoof." I laugh. "How bad is the haircut?"

"It could've been worse." Risk doesn't look concerned. "It added a little character." Risk smirks at me, and I shake my head, letting the subject drop. "My sister should be here by dinnertime tomorrow night," my husband reminds me. Jessie is a lifesaver. When my stomach started expanding at a scary rate, she offered to come and stay for a week to visit Logan and give me a break.

"Great." I yawn and fight to stay awake.

"Let's get you to bed before you turn into a pumpkin." He helps me up and leads me to the bathroom.

"Sounds like heaven," I tell him and reach for my toothbrush.

"No, heaven was what I found the day I met you." He kisses the back of my neck.

Melted. I'm a melted, blubbering mess. Only my hot, overprotective biker could turn me into a pile of goo with a few words. We are a match made in heaven.

THE END OF RISK'S REGRET

Thank you so much for reading *Risk's Regret*. I hope you enjoyed the story and will consider leaving a review.

If you'd like to read Bender and London's story, *The Rockstar* is available now.

She roars into my life and turns everything upside down.

I grumble but agree when my MC President asks for a favor. His little sister needs to interview my bassist, and he'd like me to arrange it. Little do I know, my good deed will drop her right in my lap. London Montoya is the most stunning woman I've ever seen. And she's mine. I'll do whatever it takes to keep the curvy angel for life. Cash Montoya might not like one of his MC brothers dating his little sister, but he'll just have to get over it. Nothing will stop me from making her mine.

Holy cow on steroids. Declan "Bender" Valentine is the bombdotcom. I got a sneak peek at the hot rockstar at my brother's wedding but I was too scared to approach him. That's not true. One look at him and my stupid heart and body melted. Since there's no way I stand a chance with one of the sexiest men alive, I decide to avoid him at all costs. Too bad, my best friend and boss wants me to interview his bassist for our magazine and she won't take no for an answer.

The Rockstar has his work cut out for him, but he'll do whatever it takes to make London his. He might have to go head-to-head with his best friend, but nothing will stand in his way. He's going to keep London for life even if he has to turn his entire world upside down to do it.

These wealthy Texans have it all—Money, looks, power, their MC and brothers. The only thing missing is someone to share it all with. There's a shortage of eligible ladies in town but these determined men won't let that slow them down. These MC brothers are going to turn the town of Silver Spoon Falls, Texas, on its ear looking for their curvy, soulmates.

Nichole Rose and Loni Ree are bringing you the Silver Spoon MC Series and these aren't your typical MC romance stories. Nichole and Loni like to keep things light. Come along with us on this wild instalove ride.

Hawk Knightley's story, Risky Business, will be available on July 19, 2022.

'm known in the entertainment industry as the guy who takes the biggest risks and reaps the biggest rewards. There's only one risk I refuse to take—mixing business with pleasure.

The universe has other plans in store for me though when it throws the curvy little spitfire right in my path. One look at her and I'm ready to toss my rules right out the window and make her mine, whatever it takes.

Who cares if my record label does business with her family? I don't. She's worth it.

Who cares if she's almost half my age? I don't. Age is just a number.

Who cares if she is way too perfect for me? I don't. I'll do whatever it takes to make sure she doesn't regret loving me.

Who cares if the media will have a field day with our relationship? I don't. When she stole my heart, the little angel sealed her fate. I'm ready to let the whole world will know the sassy beauty is all mine.

There's only one little fly in my ointment—her family. If her overprotective father finds out I'm about to corrupt his little girl, things will get sticky but that's a risk I'm willing to take. After all, Risky Business is my middle name.

JOIN MY READER'S GROUP

FIND OUT ABOUT MY NEW RELEASES, SALES AND OTHER PROMOTIONS.

Facebook Group (Hot Heroes and Happy Endings)

JOIN MY NEWSLETTER

GET HOW TO LOVE A HEARTBREAKER WHEN YOU SUBSCRIBE TO MY NEWSLETTER

Loni Ree Romance Newsletter

ALSO BY LONI REE

Find all my books on my website:

https://www.hotheroesandhea.com/

SILVER SPOON MC

The CEO

MONSTERS & CURVES

Mr. Nice Guy

First Bite

CELESTIAL FALLS

Cupcakes & Brimstone

Honey & Growls

Hexes & Howls

Whiskers & Wings

Glitz & Growls

Defying Roderick (Related to Celestial Falls)

CURVY CUTIES

Jenna

Emery

BOSS FROM HELL

Over It

Into It

WILD ACES

Spade's Queen

Barrett's Play

Snow's Spell (connected characters)

MEN OF VALOR MC

First Ride

FIELDING-STONE SERIES

Blindsiding Mr. Quinlan

Shocking Mr. Stone

Fielding-Stone Series Boxset

LOVE AT FIRST SIGHT SERIES

Professor Maxwell

Packaged Love

Nerd Boy

Cover Model

Love at First Sight: A Four Book Collection

STANDALONE BOOKS

Hungry For Red (A Salem Experiment Book One)

Finding His Forever (Finding His Love Book One)

Wicked Ways (Hunky Halloween)

Falling for my Enemy

Leaping into Love (Taking the Leap Book 7)

Warm Kisses (Warming Up to Love Book 6)

FOR HER

Keeping Liberty (American Heroes Book Two)(For Her Book 1)

Ignoring the Rules (For Her Book 2)

THE MACKENZIE FAMILY INCLUDES:

KANES' KISSES SERIES

Holly Kisses

Surprise Kisses (Forever Safe Christmas Book 19)

Candy Kisses

Kane's Kisses: A Four Book Collection Boxset

Forever Kisses

SWEET BEGINNINGS

Sweet Treat

Sugar Pie

LOVING A BENNETT BOY

Mr. CEO Jerk

Mr. Director Sir

Mr. Boss Man

SPARKS IN JUNIPER

Ignite My Heart

FINDING MS. RIGHT

Claiming Ms. Off Limits

Roping Ms. Imposter

PLAYING RIORDAN

Catching Payton

Scoring Gina

FALLING HARD AND FAST

Can't Resist Her

THE MERGER

Blake's Fall

Lukas' Love

Drew's Fight

FIRSTS SERIES

First Sight

First Touch

SWEET ON YOU (CLEAN, SWEET ROMANCE)
Writing as L. Ree

Knox's Surprise (Sweet on You Book 1)

Trace's Fire (Sweet on You Book 2)

Jordan's Gift (Sweet on You Book 3)

Jason's Luck (Sweet on You Book 4)

ABOUT THE AUTHOR

Loni Ree is a very busy mom of six who loves to read, and she finds that it helps her escape the chaos of everyday life. She likes quick reads that are red-hot and on the excessive side. Writing has also been a passion of hers, and Loni decided to share the stories floating around in her mind. Her short, steamy stories are a little over the top because she believes reading should be an escape from real life. She writes about hot heroes finding their beautiful soulmates and fighting for their happy endings!

Loni also has an alternate pen name L. Ree. If you like clean, sweet romance, check out her L. Ree books.

Website: Hotheroesandhea.com
https://linktr.ee/loniree19

facebook.com / lonireeromance

twitter.com / loni_ree

instagram.com / lonireeromance

amazon.com / author / loniree

bookbub.com / authors / loni-ree

goodreads.com / LoniRee

pinterest.com / loni01013104